Sometimes life can be a real mind twister. Life gets really fun when everything goes your way. Life sometimes can make you feel like you loving a snake.

As soon as you
feel you finally
have a good
grip it sheds its
skin and slips
away. Even
after all the
signs the snake
gives us that it
doesn't want to
be held.

We still reach
for it to tame
and control.
Pointing fingers
at the snake as
if the snakes the
blame.

Looking to
others as if they
are doing any
better than we
are at the time.
People say we
are all different.
Take a trip to
the local dump.

You will see
every bodies
trash all
together
stanking. Lets
just say its a
thin line
between the
same and the
different. This
book is about
the struggle we
all have inside.

This book
should help you
shine a light on
the different
feelings of your
heart and
mind.It starts
with the same
story. You can't
get your heart to
love what your
mind may like.

And also no matter how much you know you love someone in your mind. Your heart will still love another. To be the best you can be is to put your heart and mind on the same page.

The problem is
that the name of
the fight inside
you is called the
heart vs. mind
fight. Tell me
which one do
you want to win.

Truth is many people feel they would be better off without feelings. Others feel they would be much happier if they didn't over think everything.

This is normal
the problem is
when you dont
know if you live
your life from
your heart or
your mind. Here
are some
helpful stories
that may help
you find your
way thru the
darkness of
heart vs mind.

Truth is many
people try to
look to a higher
power. Many
find themselves
saying that it
doesn't work.
Some of the
bible teachers
are full of the
big head. You
know they know
everything and
you know
nothing.

Thats the beginning of the problem and why some people never get past the first conversation with a so called saved person.

Some people in church have this way of looking down on sinners. As if they were not sinners themselves. They come to you and tell you to read the bible.

So you do and try to talk with them. Only for them to tell you the few scriptures that they learned. If you ask them about something they don't have a answer too they always say just read the bible the answer is in there.

When in need
we as people
look for real
answers that
seem to work.
Its great to pray
and worship but
understanding
the meaning of
prayer can be
the power you
need.I believe in
using everything
my higher
power has gave
me to solve my
problems.

Only after i
have used all
my energy. Only
after i has used
every thought in
my mind. Only
after i have
done as man all
i can do then
and only then
do i call my
higher power. I
believe that my
life is some of
the power that
is giving.

I also feel that
we as people
are giving all the
tools to handle
life on life's
terms.There are
some problems
that man just
can not solve.

Many things like addiction and inner issues were man as a whole are to weak to handle alone.

Thats when you call upon an higher power for help. Not just to pay a bill we all know what needs to be done to pay our bills. The problem comes when you don't pay your bills and still pray for more.

Simply your higher power is only as strong or as special as you make it to be. So i only us my higher power for special situations.

HEART

He had just
found out that
he had cancer.
He was given
only 2 weeks to
live. As he
drove away
from the office
she called. As
he told her he
noticed she
didn't seem to
care when he
told her the
news.

It made him think about their whole relationship. When he met her she was dating a gang member. They were in tenth grade and the gang member was in street school.

Every weekend
the gang
member would
try to fight him
over her.The
gang member
would win all
the fights except
for one. That
night at the
movies.He
smiled as he
turned the
corner.

The gang member ran up on him in the movies. He punched and punched the gang member. He had went to the movies to watch the karate kid. He felt if the karate kid could kick so could he.

Then it
happened he
jumping and
kicked. His foot
hit the drug
dealer right in
the face. The
drug dealer fell
to the floor
crying in pain.

He grabbed her hand and they ran all the way home. That night he lost his virginity. It was the best night of his young life. The dealer was never seen again. They dated all the way to college and went to college together.

Everything was
fine for years.
Until she sat
him down and
told him her
college teacher
was trying to fail
her if she didn't
have sex with
him.Later that
day he saw the
teacher at the
gas station.

He never was
the best fighter
in the world but
he could kick. In
an instance he
had kicked the
teacher in the
face.As the
teacher layed
there in pain he
told the teacher
to never mess
with her again.

For some
strange reason
she received an
a in that class.
Later they
finished school
and moved into
a home next to
his college
buddy and his
wife.

Moving forward years later his friends wife told him she had caught his wife and her husband together.She even said she heard them talking about how the kids was his and not yours.

In his mind he
felt like killing
both of them.
He was thinking
about all the
fights he had
because of
her.He really
wanted to
dexter her
bad.Then his
heart spoke and
said you love
her. In his heart
he knew he
loved her.

He stayed quiet
even after his
friends wife left
her husband.He
stayed true to
his heart. He
never said a
word to her
ever. Soon the
cancer came
calling.

As he layed on
his death bed
he told her, i
did,i do , and i
always will love
you no matter
what. Before
she could say a
word back
silence filled the
room. Tears fell
from her eyes
and then a
pause in her
look. Her face
looked strange.

She couldn't breathe.She fell to the floor beside his bed.She tried to reach for the oxygen mask on his face. As she reached the words don't touch me came to her mind i guess cause she stopped reaching for the mask.

She then feel
dead. I know
this cause i was
watching the
camera feed in
his room. You
see im a
security guard
in the hospital
and yes im his
college buddy.

I was wrong and
never could tell
him. She was
evil and now I'm
going to have to
answer why i
didn't try to help
her. They might
put me in jail but
at least he will
be at peace.

For you see he
never did
anything to us
we did it all to
him and we
deserve we
deserve......Her
body layed
there dead. The
buddy locked in
a room
answering
questions.

He was laying
on the bed and
then the
machine went
back to
beeping. Damn
he's still alive!!!!

We all have had
the I just don't
give a damn
feeling in their
mind. At the
same time your
heart is hurting.
Or your heart is
filled with love
but your mind
says leave.

I would sit on a
bus stop bench
and wonder why
I cared for
people that
seemed to be
happy with the
thought of me
being dead.Y'all
these people
would talk about
me like I was
the left side of a
piece of shit.

They made me
feel as if I
wasn't even
good enough to
be the whole
piece of shit. I
would walk to
work everyday.
It rained some
of those days.

I swear it
seemed like the
cars would drive
close to the
curb just to
make the water
hit me.

It seemed like
on the city bus
everybody
would frown
when the only
open seat on
the bus was
beside me.
Tried to cut my
arm and die one
night while
drinking.

It felt like even
the grim reaper
frowned and
said he not
coming with me
when my blood
on my arm
started clotting
up and wouldn't
come out. Man I
just cleaned
myself up and
went to bed.

Twenty minutes
later my damn
bed fell to the
floor. The leg of
the bed had
broke. I just
looked at it and
leaned over and
slept side ways.

There was even
a tree outside
my apartment
that had an owl
that would make
a sound every
time a person
walked up to the
tree.
Then one day
when I walked
up to the tree
the damn owl
turned its head
the other way.

In my mind i
was like that's it
I just don't give
a damn
anymore. In my
heart I was hurt
because even
the owl didn't
make a sound.

We will get back
to that later lets
talk about God
and some of the
bible stories a
little.If God told
you that you
can enter
heaven but no
one you ever
loved or was
friends with
would be able to
go would you
still enter?

If you won the
lottery would
you really
share. If having
more than one
wife or husband
wasn't against
the law would
you still have
only one.

If killing wasn't
a crime would
you kill
everyday just to
release stress.
Never look
down on
yourself for the
mistakes you
have done in
your life.

Cause others
may seem like
they better
people than you
but their closet
may have a
storage unit to
hold all their
issues. Now in
my mind I
learned and
read.

Let's start with the bible. Good old moses and the staff that turned to a snake. I wanted to learn that power so I read every bible and every book. I could not find any magic trick that could turn a stick to a snake.

So I decided to
look into the
snake and work
backwards.
When moses
threw the stick it
hit the ground
and turned into
a snake.

Well looking
backwards can
a snake turn
into a stick then
I google it and
yes there is a
snake that as a
defense stiffens
up like a stick.
The snake is
called erpeton
tentaculatum,
the indonesia
tentacled snake.
These snakes
love wet mud.

Now when we
met moses he
was stomping
straw into mud.
Now what if
moses picked
up the snake in
the mud cause
he thought it
was a stick.

Then learned it
was a snake.
First it scared
him but as any
man working in
mud he must
have seen a
way to get out
the mud.

Knowing no one
had seen
anything like
that before he
came up with a
plan to become
a king with that
snake well stick.
In order to be a
king he would
need people .

I guess he said
what the hell
take the people
from the king
that had him
working in the
mud.

He probably
didn't like him
anyway. Now
this is where
heart vs mind
comes into play.
I know what all
the clues say.
Yes it may have
been a snake
that can stiffen
itself like a
snake..

It my mind I'm
saying all that
maybe true. In
my heart i still
honor my god
and choose to
believe his
story.

See no matter
snake or stick
moses is the
story of a man
with nothing that
wanted more for
his life. He had
to fight the
powers that be
and he wasn't
empty handed.

So if you found
a snake that
looked like a
stick while
working as a
slave in the mud
wouldn't you try
to trick the king
too!
 Hey in your
heart you
maybe happy if
the snake didn't
bite you.

In your mind
you probably
would be trying
to think of ways
to use it to your
advantage if
you smart.
Cause even a
snake can lend
you a hand
every now and
then.

That reminds of this guy who worked in a restaurant. See he was college educated. He had went to the job interview and the manager told him he was great for the job.

He then said he was go cross train him on every position so one day he could become a manager. The guy felt he was on his way to becoming a manager. He worked the drive thru window. He worked the cash register.

He ran the grill
doing noon rush
hour. He
opened and he
closed. He
worked days
when the
manger would
be off. He knew
all the codes.
He had his on
keys to the
store.

He also was still
making the
same wage he
was making
when he
started. Others
would get hired
after him and
given more
money for doing
only one
position.

It started to
make him mad.
He asked about
a raise and was
told the
company wasn't
doing good
enough to give
out raises.

Week after week he would watch the manager sit in the lobby doing a rush while he ran drive thru, the grill, and answer the phones. Well the word was that the district manager was coming to check the store.

The manager
told him that he
was counting on
him to make
him look good.

The general
manager came
to the store
when only he
was working
and not the
manager. The
general
manager was
impressed.

The next day
him and the
manager and
general
manager would
all be working
together.
He knew if he
did his best the
mangers lazy
ways wouldn't
be noticed by
the general
manager.

He didn't wanna look bad either after doing a great job. So on his way to work he stopped at a store. He then purchased some allergy pills.

As he walked in
the lobby of the
job he grabbed
a drink and sat
down waiting for
his shift to start.
He could see
the general
manager
shaking the
managers lazy
hand.

One by one he began to take the pills. He knew he couldn't call out of work. He knew he couldn't put on a bad work performance. He also knew that allergy pills causes drowsiness.

He felt with a little acting he could convince them to let him go.I guess I should call him moses. Anyway he clocked in and the pills started working fast.

He had took to
many of the pills
and fell to the
floor. They
called the
ambulance to
help him.
They took him
to the hospital.
He had the next
day off of work.
When he
returned to work
the general
manager was
still there.

The general
manager told
him he needed
to talk to him
before he
clocked in for
work.

The general
manager asked
him if he made
him a manager
could he count
on him. He told
him yes but
asked what
about the other
manager.

The general manager looked at him and said what other manager as he pushed the lobby doors open like the parting of the red sea. He was manager now and it was his store and his crew.

He then ran towards the lobby yelling wait do I get a raise. I smiled and clocked in!!!!

MIND

I was sitting on the beach one late night. I loved getting some beer and watching the waves. I never had a blanket so I would get the bag out of the trash can that was next to the bathroom.

I would always
scare the
people having
sex in the
bathroom when
I would push the
trash can over.
Two people
would come
running out
every time half
dressed. So
anyway I would
always sit in
front of a tree.

See the tree
blocked the
view of the cars
passing by
there. I was
drinking at night
when the beach
was closed. So
the cops could
arrest you if
they saw you.
Well unless they
could see
around trees I
would always
be okay.

While sitting
one night
listening to the
dock of the bay
and half drunk I
saw a man in
the water. He
wasn't
swimming
although he was
walking.

He was not on
the edge he
was about thirty
feet out in the
water and I
could see his
knees. Well the
first thing I said
was oh hell here
come Jesus. I
went to turning
the beer up can
after can.

I didn't want any
beer to be
around me
when Jesus
walked up. So I
drunk it all really
fast. As I was
drinking the
second beer the
guy went down
in the water it
was to his neck.

I stood up and
said to myself
damn Jesus
drowning.
Man I had on
new clothes and
wanted to dive
in but I was
thinking about
how much my
shirt costed.
Then I felt
Jesus would
dive in and save
me so I headed
to the water
beer in hand.

Then the guy
stood up and
walked out the
water. I asked
are you okay.
He said yes I'm
fine. Now the
beer made me
feel as if I was
standing there
talking to Jesus.
So then I said to
him I just saw
you walking on
water.

He smiled and
said yes in
some waters
they have what
you call a shoal.
Some call it a
sandbank or
sandbar. During
high tide you
won,t see it at
all. During low
tides the water
level drops and
if you swim out
to it you can
walk on it.

He then said well enjoy your night. He then walked behind the building where you take showers. About five minutes later I heard a car start.

It was coming
from behind that
same building.
Then a car
started coming
from behind the
building it was a
cop car. At that
moment I was
stiff as that tree.
Until the car
slowed down
and a waving
hand came out
the window.

It was the same
guy so I waved
back to him. I
didn't move or
take my eyes
off the car till I
couldn't see the
tail lights
anymore.Then
the wind went to
blowing. A wave
of water hit my
foot.

I felt like a teen
being
challenged at a
fight. I felt the
water hit my
feet challenging
me to swim out
and see if I
could walk on
water. My heart
said lets do it.

My mind said
you crazy as
hell. Not to
mention I was
two shades in
the wind. Also
there are no
telephone pole
lights in the
water. Again my
heart said just
swim straight.
My mind said
what happens if
you pass by it
or swim the
wrong way.

Well I was
drinking some
good stuff. My
heart had won. I
stepped into the
water with
purpose. By
time the water
level reached
my stomach I
was moving
really slow.

I was looking
back thinking of
turning around.
Then the wind
started blowing
and between
the waves and
the wind I had
to keep going.
In an instance
the waves and
wind stopped.

The water was up to my neck. Then I felt something under me. I had been swimming in four feet of water. I stood up and looked around. I was standing in the middle of the ocean.

It was about
three in the
morning. I had
put my last two
beers in my
pocket. I
opened one and
again my heart
said lets swim
back.My mind
said nope finish
your beer and
swim back
when the sun
come up.

So what do you think I did. Even you will have moments like that between your heart and mind.
Remember the choice is yours and well as for that night. I can tell you I finished my beer!

NORTH

Mark was an
black man. He
was a blue
collar worker.
During his spare
time he liked to
drink and
smoke. He lived
in an northern
city in an
northern state.

On the north part of town. His lady was a sweet women. She went to church every Sunday. One sunday she asked Mark a question. The question was a simple one.

She asked if
God told you
that you could
enter heaven
but no one you
ever loved or
ever was friends
with could go
would you still
enter the gates
of heaven.

Mark was sitting in an old chair he had found beside the road. He was watching an television that he had found in an dumpster next to a rental store. He looked at her and said that he had two feelings about her question.

He then said
well my first
feeling is that in
my mind we all
wanna go to
heaven. He said
that all his life
he was raised to
obey god. He
looked around
and said so in
my mind I would
enter.

Then he said
my second
feeling about
your question
comes from my
heart. He then
said even
though it is
heaven how
happy would I
be without
having some if
not only one
person I loved
there.

It would be like
getting rich and
having no one
to share your
money with. He
then asked her
a question. He
asked do you
think everyone
that God picks
to go to heaven
will go. She
replied saying
yes.

He smiled and said everyone with a concert ticket doesn't always go to the concert. People with season tickets to the ball games may never see a game. People with God's blessing also may say no.

Cause even
going to heaven
is an choice. He
then said your
answer is
maybe.
Depends on
how life turns
out to be in his
last days he
said. Then he
said with a
smile after life
without you just
won't do!

South

John was an white man. He was a white collar worker. During his spare time he liked to drink and smoke. He lived in an southern city in an southern state. On the southern part of town.

His lady was a
sweet women.
She went to
church every
Sunday. One
sunday she
asked john a
question.

The question
was a simple
one. She asked
if God told you
that you could
enter heaven
but no one you
ever loved or
ever was friends
with could go
would you still
enter the gates
of heaven.

John was sitting
in an chair he
had payed for
online.He was
watching an
television that
he had found at
an rental store.
He looked at
her and said
that he had two
feelings about
her question.

He then said
well my first
feeling is that in
my mind we all
wanna go to
heaven. He said
that all his life
he was raised to
obey god. He
looked around
and said so in
my mind I would
enter.

Then he said
my second
feeling about
your question
comes from my
heart. He then
said even
though it is
heaven how
happy would I
be without
having some if
not only one
person I loved
there.

It would be like getting rich and having no one to share your money with. He then asked her a question. He asked do you think everyone that God picks to go to heaven will go. She replied saying yes.

He smiled and
said everyone
with a concert
ticket doesn't
always go to the
concert. People
with season
tickets to the
ball games may
never see a
game.

People with
God's blessing
also may say
no. Cause even
going to heaven
is an choice. He
then said your
answer is i dont
know. Depends
on how life turns
out to be in his
last days he
said.

Then he said
with a smile
after life without
you just won't
do!

East

Luke was an red man. He was a migrant worker. During his spare time he liked to drink and smoke. He lived in an eastern city in an eastern state. On the eastern part of town.

His lady was a
sweet women.
She went to
church every
Sunday. One
sunday she
asked luke a
question.

The question
was a simple
one. She asked
if God told you
that you could
enter heaven
but no one you
ever loved or
ever was friends
with could go
would you still
enter the gates
of heaven.

Luke was
sitting in an
chair that
someone had
given him. He
was watching
an television
that he had
found at an thrift
store.

He looked at
her and said
that he had two
feelings about
her question.
He then said
well my first
feeling is that in
my mind we all
wanna go to
heaven. He said
that all his life
he was raised to
obey god.

He looked
around and said
so in my mind I
would enter.
Then he said
my second
feeling about
your question
comes from my
heart.

He then said
even though it is
heaven how
happy would I
be without
having some if
not only one
person I loved
there. It would
be like getting
rich and having
no one to share
your money
with.

He then asked her a question.He asked do you think everyone that God picks to go to heaven will go. She replied saying yes.

He smiled and said everyone with a concert ticket doesn't always go to the concert. People with season tickets to the ball games may never see a game. People with God's blessing also may say no.

Cause even
going to heaven
is an choice. He
then said your
answer is no I
wouldn't enter.
Then he said
with a smile
after life without
you would be
sad.

West

Matthew was an
yellow man. He
was a seasonal
worker. During
his spare time
he liked to drink
and smoke. He
lived in an
western city in
an western
state. On the
western part of
town.

His lady was a
sweet women.
She went to
church every
Sunday. One
sunday she
asked Matthew
a question.

The question
was a simple
one. She asked
if God told you
that you could
enter heaven
but no one you
ever loved or
ever was friends
with could go
would you still
enter the gates
of heaven.

Matthew was sitting in an chair that he had stolen. He was watching an television that he had stolen. He looked at her and said that he had two feelings about her question.

He then said
well my first
feeling is that in
my mind we all
wanna go to
heaven. He said
that all his life
he was raised to
obey god. He
looked around
and said so in
my mind I would
enter.

Then he said
my second
feeling about
your question
comes from my
heart. He then
said even
though it is
heaven how
happy would I
be without
having some if
not only one
person I loved
there.

It would be like getting rich and having no one to share your money with. He then asked her a question. He asked do you think everyone that God picks to go to heaven will go. She replied saying yes.

He smiled and said everyone with a concert ticket doesn't always go to the concert. People with season tickets to the ball games may never see a game.

People with
God's blessing
also may say
no. Cause even
going to heaven
is an choice. He
then said your
answer is yes i
would enter.

Then he said
with a smile
after life without
you would be
sad but the
angels in
heaven would
dry my tears.All
four men did
have things in
common. Two
was answering
the question
with their mind.

Two were
answering from
the heart.
If you were
asked that
question how
would you
respond. Would
you enter
heaven alone?

JUMPING
THRU
DARKNESS
BOOK ONE
AND TWO
RECAP
ALCOHOLIC
ROAD
This is all just a
suggestion. I
noticed that
every book from
the bible to the
big a.a book
tells you if you
do these steps it
will work.

To me the
overlooked part
of that is that we
are all different
and what works
for some does
not always work
for others.

The twelve
steps for you
may take all
twelve but for
your friend it
may only take
two steps.
 I remember
going to
meeting and
while there
listening to the
stories how
much I really
needed a drink.

I would leave a
meeting about
not drinking and
go get drunk. I
would hear
stories of crime
and how bad it
could get and
say to myself , I
don't do those
things hell I am
fine then.

I would
compare the
things in my life
with the stories
of other
alcoholics. My
story was
nowhere near
as bad.

Therefore my alcoholic mind said hay we okay then. we can drink more we not as bad as we thought. As I would walk to the store I would be dressed and smelling good. My hair cut and face shaved.

My bills would
be and always
be paid. So I felt
if anyone could
have a drink
well I could. As I
would get near
the store I
would notice
men and
woman around
the store.

Some of them looked as if they were homeless. As I would get near the store I would notice men and woman around the store. Some of them looked as if they were homeless.

Some even
looked as if they
found the secret
to life,which was
why go to the
bathroom just
do it in your
clothes. All of
these people
had the same
object near
them or in their
hands.

Now neither
person had the
same inside but
they all had the
same brown
paper bag.
At the time I
never noticed
that i left the
store with one
of those objects
and even the
famous brown
paper bag.

I know even you
have hung out
with the famous
Mr brown bag a
few times.
Needless to say
a brown bag
was important
to me for a good
time as votes
are to an
election.

How do you say
it ain't fun if you
ain't drunk.
Things you say
on alcoholic
road.

Drinking
partners

Some times
your friends can
play a part in
your drinking.
They can help
you to drink
more than you
should. Friends
will challenge
you to drink
more and more.

Never caring if you drink to much. Most say the drunker the better. They will be right there drunk and fighting when trouble starts. If two friends have two dollars and fifty cents.

They both have
five dollars for a
six pack of beer.
Let me tell you
about a
situation I went
thru while
drinking and
living in a
rooming house.

A rooming house is where single people can rent a room in a house. It was a Friday night.

I was broke
because I had A
get paid every
two weeks type
of job. That
week just wasn't
my pay week.
So I was bored
and wanted to
party. I heard a
knock on the
door it was my
friend creepy
dude.

I tell you that
his Nick name
was creepy
dude no lie. He
said hay man
you always give
me drinks when
you have some
well tonight I'm
get you drunk.

I smiled finally
all that give a
drunk a beer
one day they
will give you
one stuff
worked. I said to
him cool cause I
need some.He
said okay give
me thirty
minutes and I'll
be back.

Now I didn't
believe in
private drinking
in my room with
men. I only
drink alone with
women. So I
grabbed my
radio and some
chairs from the
kitchen. Put a
table outside
the front door.

I then went to
my room and
grabbed a deck
of cards.
I was broke but
creepy dude
had drinks and
the
neighborhood
had plenty
gamblers.

Let's just say I didn't plan on being broke for long. I turned on the radio and stood up and looked around. Imagine a zoo now imagine a zoo when a the gates unlock all at once. Okay now picture the animals that walk to the gate and look out.

Can you see the look of happiness and hope.
Well standing on my porch that's what it seemed like when I turned the music on. I saw people peeping out windows and doors smiling.

First person that
walked over
was airwick .
We called him
airwick because
smoke came
out his mouth
even when he
wasn't smoking.
Then came vet
she was thick
and loud and
always had a
dress on.

I should
mention that a
dress is the only
piece of clothing
she would wear.
If you never saw
a woman's body
vet would lift
that dress and
explain every
part.

We called her
vet cause she
always told sex
stories. She
would always
end a story with
I have done
every position
wanna learn
more. At that
moment creepy
dude pulled up
in a trunk filled
with drinks.

He had a keg of
beer. He had a
box of wine with
about twelve
bottles in it also.
He had burgers
and a real damn
pig on the truck.
He looked at me
and said I gat
us some for too.

Now me
,vet,and airwick
all said who in
the hell go cook
a pig. Vet then
said his dumb
ass. Creepy
dude said fine
I'll cook him
bring me some
gas. I looked
like what the
hell did he just
say.

Well the party started and we were having a ball. Airwick kept trying to smoke up my cigarettes. Vet kept trying to get me alone in the house so she could show me her new panties.

Who she fooling
everyone knows
she done wear
any. I had just
started to feel
the affect of the
beer when the
cops pulled up.
It was like they
was
everywhere. I
swear it seemed
like one parked
on the roof.

I heard
everybody get
on the ground.
Vet screamed
out I don't have
on panties.
Someone
screamed back
we know now
on the ground.

Well I was to
dressed to get
dirty. So being
the smartest at
the party I felt I
should ask a
question. Now
the alcohol
inside me
changed the
words. I meant
to a ask what's
the problem
officers.

What came out
was do y'all
know how to
cook a pig.
Someone
screamed they
don't eat meat.
We all was on
the ground then
cause we all
was laughing
over butts off.

The officer that walked over to us was laughing himself. He then looked at me and asked do you know anything about a robbery. I said what robbery. He sad someone robbed the shopping center grocery and liquor store.

He then said
that they even
stole a pig from
the meat
market. I tired to
play it off so I
said I haven't
seen any pigs.
Vet looked at
me and said hell
I see a lot of
them .

Now airwick
who by this time
was sitting at
the table
smoking my
cigarettes sad it
was that man
that lived at the
church. He said
that man said
he was cleaning
the world by
stealing swine
and all the wine.

The cops left us
alone and
people was
walking by
talking we want
bacon or we tell.
When things gat
quiet I asked
where the hell is
creepy and the
pig.

So we went to
creepy's room
opened the
door.Creepy
was in bed with
pig. I asked
what the hell
creepy, he said
if they would
have knocked
on my door I
would have told
them it was our
honeymoon.

I knew then that
I should drink
alone cause
some people
have more
issues than
drinking.

The only holiday
drink method

Here is one
way that helped
me with
drinking. I said
to myself that
drinking every
weekend was to
much. I tried
just to stop all at
once.

I found myself drinking more after a week or two. I then decided to add meanings to my drinking. Like special occasions like my birthday or everyone's birthday.

Well if you
have a lot of
friends then
that's a lot of
drinking. I
needed
occasions that
stayed the
same. I then
noticed the
calendar on the
wall.

Its like ten
major holidays
in a year give or
take depends
on what you like
to celebrate. I
then said I
would only drink
on holidays.

At first I felt I would not make it but I did. From new years I didn't drink anything until valentines day. I felt great and had a ball. I was able to control myself and enjoy myself.

The test was
the next day
when I had
some beers left
over. I quickly
poured them
down the drain.
I was on to the
next holiday
with the same
system in place.

What a surprise
I made it and
was working
what I like to
call holiday
limits. For me I
went from
drinking every
weekend to
drinking only
twelve times in
one year.

I guess you can say I was working my own twelve step program. I felt great and with me knowing that I could drink on holidays I didn't feel the need to drink every weekend.

I did these steps for almost two years. The second year I even picked holidays and didn't drink bringing my count down to less than eight for the year. Now this was just the physical method to stopping drinking so much.

I soon learned that drinking also have a mental aspect to it, that I soon found out was not as easy to conquer.Okay lets get back to the topic of this book heart vs mind.

LOVE

One thing that
holds true for all
is that everyone
of us tends to
wish for that
fairytale
moment. Like
the love scene
in movies.

We all at one time in life has imagined ourselves in one or more love scenes. The music is playing you say your lines the other person says their line. It ends with a lovable moment.

I can remember
wanting to be
Dewayne from
its a different
world. As he ran
in the wedding
saying baby
please. Whitley
leaving Byron to
run to
dewayne's
arms.

Yeap I played the Dewayne part in my head everytime a woman left another guy for me. Only thing is in life you often get to play every role. So yes I have had to play the part of Byron some also!

I found myself in
love with the
way I loved.
See it was
never about
how fine or sexy
the girl was to
me. I fell in love
with the words I
would say and
the attitudes I
used to make
them love me
more.

I have even told
them its really
not about them
making me love.
I would tell them
I love them
cause I want to
love them. I
would say
things like its
not your body.
It's not your sex.

It's none of those things because as we get older those things are the first to go. So I would tell them that I loved them cause they needed to be loved.

In my mind
loving someone
that needed to
be loved was
greater than
loving someone
that had all the
love in the
world, and your
love was just
another love to
them.

If we are truly to
be Christ like
then loving is
also a weapon.
God, Jesus or
who ever you
call him big
dude upstairs
chooses to love
us because he
wants too.

Jesus didn't
have to show us
the way and
give his life for
us. Jesus
wanted to trade
his life to free
another. Jesus
wanted
everyone to see
him suffer so
that they could
feel gods love
and know that it
is real.

Jesus choose to love us no matter the cost. So I look at love between two people the same way. You can't ever feel what's in another person's heart.

You can be with
a person twenty
years and never
know how they
really feel. Many
try to explain
their feelings so
the other can
relate to them.

So if you can't feel what your lover feels then what are you in love with in the first place. That's right you are really in love with yourself. You feel that inside. Your heart loves the way you talk to your lover.

Your heart loves
the way you act
with your
lover.It's not the
other person
filling your heart
its you yourself.
Your heart loves
how in your
mind you are
happy.

So your heart
tries to match
the happiness in
your mind with
emotions. We
know these
emotions to be
called love. So
your heart feels
you with great
feelings that
help strengthen
the happiness in
your mind.

Now the mind
can sometimes
fall for the
wrong thing.
Causing the
heart to love
something it
doesn't. These
battle of
emotions cause
anger,pain,
sadness,etc.

The heart often gives its all for you to feel the love emotions when it thinks you are happy. When the heart finds out you are no longer happy it tries to empty the love emotions quickly.

This causes
pain and stress
to the heart. It
makes the body
weak. It makes
the body sad.
Cause what's
the other side of
happiness.

Nevertheless
your heart and
mind does all
the work when it
comes to love.
So stop giving
your credit
away. Say you
love them cause
you want too. If
you are happy
with them its
because you
want to be.

If you are not
happy with them
its because you
want to be.
Love starts in
the mind. If in
your mind you
like something
soon your heart
will make you
love it! So I love
for me is what
you should be
saying.

Tuned up

Choosing to
take the pain in
your heart and
move forward
can be hard.
Sometimes it
hurts to do the
right thing. Even
when the right
thing leaves you
a broken heart.

I often compare
the heart and
mind to car
parts. The front
of the car is the
brain. The life of
the car is the
gas. Neither
one will work
very well
without the
other.

Okay so in your
mind you want
to be a dancer.
The problem
with that is in
your heart you
really don't like
it as much as
you may think.
You don't
practice. You do
the dances just
good enough to
finish the song.

One would say
that your heart
isn't in it. So in
my terms you
don't have the
gas. Even if the
battery in the
car is full of
power and
ready to ride.

You won't be
going anywhere
without any gas.
So no matter
what is in your
mind it's only as
good as what's
in your heart.
The trick is to
tune up your
heart and mind
to work
together.

One way to do
this is to find
something you
know you love.
Have a seat and
just look at or
think about
nothing but that
thing you know
you love.

Try to forever forget everything else in your life that you truly don't love. Then start adding only things that you know you love in your life. No more maybe type of people. No more its a okay job.

No more I like
them but don't
love them
relationships.
When you shop
only buy what
you love and
not what
someone else
likes for you.
Deal with
nothing but
things that
make you
happy.

You won't be
going anywhere
without any gas.
So no matter
what is in your
mind it's only as
good as what's
in your heart.
The trick is to
tune up your
heart and mind
to work
together.

One way to do
this is to find
something you
know you love.
Have a seat and
just look at or
think about
nothing but that
thing you know
you love.

Sometimes it
can seem as if
your mind has a
mind of its own.
Many people
have had their
mind think
about their ex
while they are
happy in
another
relationship.

The mind tends
to have its own
agenda
sometimes.
That's when
your heart
should step in
for you to clear
those
misunderstood
and out of place
thoughts.

If you do the tune up right you should be able to look at yourself from within yourself and examine everything. You should be able to see your own thoughts and feelings.

You should be
then able to pick
what thoughts
and emotions
that are relevant
for you and your
life. Remember
the heart
doesn't see
what the eyes
see. The heart
doesn't feel
what the body
feels.

The heart gets
the thoughts
that comes from
the mind and
adds emotions.
So learn to keep
you mind on an
always loving
treatment.
Doing that will
put your heart
on an always
loving
treatment.

Leading you to
an positive
outlook on love
and life without
regrets.

The exercise

Let's define what's in your mind compared to what's in your heart. Grab a blank piece of paper. Grab a piece of paper with words on it.

Take the piece
of paper with
words on it and
destroy it
because it has
the story of the
old you on it.
Now look at the
blank piece of
paper and write
down all the
things you love
from your heart
on the paper.

Now get
another piece of
blank paper and
with your mind
write all the
things that you
can think of that
make you
happy. Now
compare the
two papers.
Make sure you
are honest.

Let's change
the topic for
awhile so you
can focus on
writing. I like
me. I like me. I
like me. Okay
that's enough
brain tune up
for me. Let's
see how you did
with your
papers. Did they
almost match.

Well if both
papers don't
have the exact
things on it your
mind and heart
may not be on
the same page.
Remember in
order to really
love your heart
and mind must
be in tune. See
if its something
on your papers
that need work.

Also look at
those things on
your mind page
and wonder why
it makes you
happy but you
don't have it on
your love page.
Now that you
have the two
papers get
another blank
one and look at
it.

From your heart
write about why
someone
should love you.
Now get one
more paper
don't worry I
won't ask again.
Okay from your
mind now write
all the reasons
someone
shouldn't love
you.

Now look at
both papers and
wonder why the
two look like the
other side of
each other. Like
on your heart
page you said
someone
should love you
cause you
communicate
well. Now on
your mind page
you wrote you
talk to much.

Get my meaning. Fine tuning the heart and mind in an lifetime task. Don't think that it's a one and done type of thing. You should always reach for a new sheet in life. End of exercise!

Sound mind

In my heart I am
truly happy for
all the people
that seem to
have won their
fights. Those
fighting to get
some drugs
legal. Many
people truly
need certain
drugs to
function.

So in my heart I am happy for them. In my mind I'm looking around and see more people being added to the list of people on drugs.

Between the
Molly and the
other pill
poppers the
numbers of
people that
minds are under
the influence
are adding up
fast.Most
people you
meet are on
something.

It maybe pain
pills or it maybe
pills for some
kind of
sickness.
Others use
weed or liquid
weed. Many use
alcohol and pills
and weed.

It makes me
wonder how
many people
are left that truly
don,t use
anything to
make it day to
day.Add in the
rise in crime
and lack of work
makes the
streets become
filled with
addicts of all
nature and
ages.

The drugs then
are in the driver
seat. It maybe
affecting
everyone even
our leaders.
Now to do Any
drug is your
choice but
everything has
a price.

For example there once was a guy named Steven. Steven lived alone on the first floor. His apartment was the fourth door down on the right from the entrance door. He once dated a stripper that no one had seen around for weeks.

It was early one morning when a thump at the door woke steven up. He climbed out of bed. He looked around and saw all in his place was good. The dishes were clean.The floor was clean.

His television was on but not loud. He walked into the bathroom and looked around. Everything was in place in the bathroom. He opened his dresser and pulled out pants. He reached in his closet and grabbed a shirt.

Within an hour
Steven was
dressed and
smiling.
He then walked
over to the
couch and had
a seat. The
sounds of his
stripper
girlfriend saying
he looked good
made him smile.

He turned up
the television
when a special
report can on
about an twenty
six year old
woman still
missing after
three weeks.

The missing
woman,s name
was Stacy jetta
and she was
last seen
leaving her
apartment.
Steven heard
his girlfriend say
that was a
shame.

His girlfriend
told him she
was hungry. So
Steven said
okay baby I will
fix us some
breakfast.
Steven rocked
and rolled in the
kitchen. After he
was finished the
two plates were
filled with eggs,
sausage,
bacon, biscuits,
and grits.

As he was
eating he
noticed his
girlfriend had
not eaten
anything. He
asked babe I
cooked this
cause you said
you was hungry.

He then heard
her say I'm
hungry for some
more feel good.
Feel good is
what they both
called the drugs
they used.
Steven said I
will be right
back. He ran
out the door and
up the street.

As he was walking he noticed a bird sitting on the stop sign. He began to shake cause that bird was watching him mighty hard. As soon as the bird flew away Steven began to walk faster.

He was almost
at peace until a
cat ran from
under a car he
was passing by
on the sidewalk.
He jumped over
two garbage
cans and ran
around the
corner. He had
arrived at the
spot.

He pulled a
hundred dollar
bill out his
pocket. He also
pulled an empty
drug bag out of
his pocket.

He was
standing in front
of an apartment
that had one
window boarded
on the left and
one window
with a hand
sized hole to the
right.

Steven walked over to the window and stuck the empty drug bag and money in the hole in the window. Steven then bent over to tie his shoes.

After he finished
with his shoes
he reached into
the hole in the
window and
pulled out a full
new bag of
drugs. Steven
put the drugs in
his pocket and
ran all the way
back home.

After hours of
drug use the
television news
was still running
an ad for the
missing woman.
He heard his
girlfriend say
she was sleepy.
He said fine he
would get some
sleep also.

Then there was an knock at the door and then the door was kicked in. Five armed police ran inside the apartment. They yelled to Steven get on the floor. They arrested Steven and began to take him outside to the police car.

Steven was
screaming
nobody better
bother my
girlfriend.
Steven heard
her voice
screaming I love
you Steven.

A week later the judge told Steven his charges.Steven couldn't believe when the judge said murder. He said I was just getting high with my girl friend. See a month ago Steven had went to a strip club where he met Stacy jetta.

She gave him
her number and
told him to get
some drugs for
later and she
would come
over.

The last time
she was seen
was going to his
place. When
she arrived they
sat on the
couch and
watched
television. She
told him she
was hungry and
he told her all
he had was
breakfast food.

She said great
cook and I will
be getting us
both high. He
was cooking
they both were
doing drugs and
the television
was on the syfy
channel. She
took two pills
and leaned
back on the
couch.

Stacy died of an overdose five minutes later. Steven came out the kitchen with the food. Steven was as high as he ever had been. From what he could see she was talking to him on the couch.

Even being
dead stacy
seemed to be
alive to him
because of the
drugs. Weeks
went by and
steven stayed
high everyday.

Every
conversation
that steven was
having with
Stacy was all in
his head while
Stacy sat there
dead.

Only reason the
cops found her
is because he
was so high
when he went to
get more drugs
Steven left his
apartment door
wide open. The
smell filled the
building.

He now sits in
meeting to
explain how in
his heart he
loved her and in
his mind that
would never
stop! So I
wonder who
won the heart or
the mind?

Two worlds

Sometimes it can seem as if the world you live in is not the world you live in. Digital life allows the powers that be to control everything from your television to your computer.

They may even
be able to
control who
accepts your
friend requests
on Facebook.
Only allowing
who they want
to be on there.

For instance
you send a
friend request
and they see it
then they
become that
person and
accept the
request. So
everything you
see and do is all
them.

You ever
wonder why
every social site
is always filled
with people
from other
states.Most of
the people on
your site are
from different
cities.

When you do
send requests
to people in
your city they
don't get
accepted why is
that. That's that
control thing
you know what I
mean.

Like how many
of you go to
sleep and every
time you wake
up the phone
rings a few
minutes later.
That's that thing
you know.

Leaves you to
wonder how
much of real life
is really real. I
would often say
nothing on a
computer is
real. I would
then say only
the pictures are
real. Turns out
only a few
pictures are
even real.

I look at the web
and cell phones
and television
for what they
are to me. They
are simply
entertainment
devices.

So to me
nothing has to
ever be real
because its all
entertainment.
Never has a
computer or a
phone or even a
television ever
said everything
you see and or
hear once you
turn me on is
real.

It doesn't even
say that you
should believe
anything you
see and or hear.
That's why I say
it's just
entertainment to
me. I believe
nothing I see or
hear.

I watch and or listen. I type and or watch. I call and answer calls. I do all knowing in my mind it may not be real. In my heart I love when I get a sexy chat message on my computer.

In my heart I
love watching
my favorite
series on
television. In my
heart I love
having my
phone handy to
get those
important phone
calls.

Even though in
my heart I don't
really like
people calling
me without
purpose. I still
on the other
hand love
getting those
calls. So is any
of it really real.

I mean just to
be able to have
a phone call
and not feel like
its five people
spying on the
call. Or to walk
outside and not
feel like twenty
pictures were
took before you
took your first
step outside.

They all seem
to wonder why
Americans tend
to do evil things.
Well America
does seem to
treat Americans
like terrorists.
They monitor
ever email and
phone call.
They watch
every bank
account.

Everything is
digital and
sends usage
data to
someone
probably in
space.

Then on top of
that when you
not at home you
see local
authorities
every two
blocks watching
you. They say it
is the land of
the free. Truth is
nothing and no
one is truly free
in America.

Even the word
freedom is only
used when they
want to use it.
An even it is
locked inside a
book.

Life can make
you sometimes
feel as if it is
truly you against
the world. It
may seem as if
everybody that
looks at you has
it out for you.

As soon as you
turn your back
they are saying
all types of evil
things under
their breathes.
Even down to
the phone call
that always
seems to
happen as soon
as you walk
inside a place.

You walk in and the person behind the desk is smiling. Then as you began to talk the phone rings and the person no longer smiles. They often become nasty. So at that point they don't even wanna help you anymore.

People the
person behind
the desk isn't
the problem.
We need to get
our hands on
the caller! Some
would say you
in a world all its
own.

Like a video
game trying to
make it to the
end. Your mind
can make life
seem special.
Your mind is
strong enough
to show you two
different worlds.
One world has a
good you and a
good life.

The other world
has you and
your sins
cooking in a lot
of pity. You
would think that
you could notice
the difference
between the
two. The only
thing is both
worlds are
equal.

The only
difference is the
choices you
make in life. You
can find
yourself
hopping from
one world to
another. Like
every time
something good
happens to you
some bad is
sure to follow.

That's because
when something
good happens
most people get
bull headed and
start doing silly
things. Those
things send
them to the pity
side.

Like for instance
someone is
blessed with a
bonus at work.
They are
walking on the
good world
grounds. That
night they don't
buy food for the
house. They
don't pay any
bills.

At that point
they are leaving
the grounds of
good. They
begin to enter
the land of pity.
They take the
money and go
to a club. Now
they are walking
the grounds of
pity lane.

The club gets raided and they get arrested. That's what's happens when you venture down pity lane. Lets just say take time out to know the two worlds. It easy to find the two worlds.

Just take a left
than right and
think about the
choices you
make in life!

Reset

How often have
you been using
an computer
and it freezes.
In order to fix
the computer to
make it work
you restart it or
reset. You are
watching the
television and it
goes blank.

You check the
cable box and it
tells you to
unplug it so it
can reset.
Almost
everything in life
comes with a
reset button.

So when it
comes to dating
shouldn't
everyone reset
when they start
dating someone
new.In your
mind you meet
the new person
and they are
kind and nice to
you.

In your heart all
you can feel is
that the person
may do the
same thing your
ex did to you.
Then your mind
starts to think
things like they
did that too.

You know the
my ex laughed
just like that
thinking. I never
treat anyone the
same as the
person before
them. Mainly
because I'm
never the same
man when
starting
something new.

Something new
means just that
something new.
So I enter a new
relationship with
a new smile. I
enter a new
relationship with
new lies.

Some of you call it game. I call it lies. I enter a new relationship with different mouthwash. I enter a new relationship with a new type of body wash. I get rid of all my old underwear and buy all new ones.

I then in my
mind empty out
all thoughts of
the love I had. I
also empty out
my heart of the
feelings I once
knew.

I Reset and fill myself with the thoughts of the next woman.In my mind I slowly think about making her happy once we meet. So everyday I am thinking about the new woman.

In my heart I am
feeling the
wanting of a
new love and
not the pain of a
lost love.
Resetting can
take some time.
It is not done
over night.

So use the time
to fix the outer
parts of your life
while you work
on the inner.
Get that new
job. Paint your
bedroom. Buy
new furniture.
Give your heart
and mind the
time it needs to
reset.

When you are
ready it will
seem as if you
could be happy
alone because
you are reset.

This is just
some words to
get you to
where you are
going in life.
Remember the
mind and heart
much work
together.
Remember to
fine tune them
both from time
to time.

Most of all
invest in your
heart and mind
and watch how
lovely they both
treat you..

Thanks for
reading ,
OVERSEER